BUILD
UNIVERSES

Natasha Anderson

Metamorphosis

© 2022 **Europe Books** | London
www.europebooks.co.uk – info@europebooks.co.uk

ISBN 979-12-201-3196-4
First edition: May 2023

Metamorphosis

Dedicated to

Dad the righteous one
Mom the honest one
Pooh the unconditional loving one
Boy the admired one
Myange my closest friend
and the nightwatchman, prophet and truthteller

Acknowledgements

I would like to thank my friend Theresa Keay for typing the manuscript and for her encouragement.

I would like to thank Andrew van der Merwe for the beautiful calligraphy and scriptures.

Grateful thanks go to the Body of Christ - the Bride - and to St John's Parish, Cape Town.

This is our story.

Natasha Anderson

Metamorphosis
Modernism and
Post-Modernism

This is a fantasy
Pure fantasy
It is a dream
A dream about an old man who dies alone
And leaves a gift behind
And it is a fantasy

Neil Diamond
Morningside[1]

---

1   https://www.albumcancionyletra.com/corregir_morningside-live_
de_neil-diamond_letra__219734.aspx

"Vanity of vanities,
said the Preacher,
"Vanity of vanities,
all is vanity."

הבל

Fact

Imagination: It is "the ability to create pictures in your mind; the part of your mind that does this."
(Oxford Advanced Learner's Dictionary, 2001)

Imagination: skill, fantasy, understanding, insight, empathy, sympathy, moral sensibility, frenzy, ecstasy, inspiration, fancy, imagery, artistry, creative work.
(Longman Pocket Companions, Thesaurus, 1982)

Imagination began when I could think and express my thoughts in language, internally in my mind, even before I could actually verbalize, whilst still in my highchair. Did my mother really have to feed me those extra four spoonsful to finish the entire bowl? (Sigh!)

Yes, as young children we learn language only because we are imaginative. And because we are imaginative we learn language. Our imagination is there to help us to play and so preceded the 'real' life which we have to embrace and engage in. And through this play we are able to make sense of reality. We are able to bring about changes and movements and invent possibilities or new alternatives for ourselves.

According to the Master Class, imagination contains everything that is non-rational: compassion, intuition, dreams, wonder, love, awe, faith and truth and it is what makes us essentially human.

Fiction

One night, as I lay in our bedroom about to fall asleep, whilst there was a party in the distant lounge, the door of the bedroom opened and there stood a man in a black hat, silhouetted against the light, tall and ominous, frightening and slim. He closed the door, and I could feel the presence as he walked around the beds back and forth, back and forth, so evil and black...I was rigid with fear and too numb to scream, he was so overpowering and black, so evil – and finally I awoke.

I looked around the room. The light was filtering gently in through the blinds. All was well. The night before was behind. I was safe in my bed.

But then began the dreams and the nightmares of the bogey-man and wet beds and the fear. "Mommy, Mommy, there is a man at the window, trying to get in." "Daddy, Daddy, what is in the cupboard?" "Patty, Patty, who is under the bed?"

"Tashy, Tashy, it is the rustling of the leaves" and "Tashy, Tashy, it is your mackintosh."

And as I grew up, I could feel the pain. The pain of my brother as he hit the glass and shattered the pane into a trillion, white crystals which showered the universe. And the pain of my sister as she cried real salt for the first time. And my pain, unable to be expressed because it was too big, too frightening, too powerful, too evil... A time so dark – so desolate – so splashed – bright blue black nothingness. And I thought that I would never see Jesus again.

And thank goodness for the stories and the dreams. The stories about Cinderella and the prince where they lived happily ever after. The dreams of being the Ugly Duckling which turned into a swan. And the story about Sleeping Beauty as she slept and slept and was then awakened by the kiss.

Oh yes, thank goodness for the dreams. Without the dreams we could not have continued. Life would have been too difficult, too burdensome to carry. And my mother, so warm, so embracing, so comforting as she put her arms around me and enveloped me with gentle German crooning.

"Ich bin klein, mein Hertz is rein, soll niemand drin wohnen asl Jesus allein."

And I would lie awake at night and watch the shadows of the cars come and go, come and go, shadows of light lengthening, shortening and then slowly disappearing. And then the next and the next... And I would think and dream and imagine a world with no more shadows, only light.

I remember going to the circus and living the colours and vitality of the jolly clowns, the dancing girls with feathers, riding the prancing ponies around and around and then the ringmaster with his top hat and his whip... It was a magical world of noise and laughter and gaiety and it drew me in and stroked my fears.

קַוֵּה תּוֹלֶת

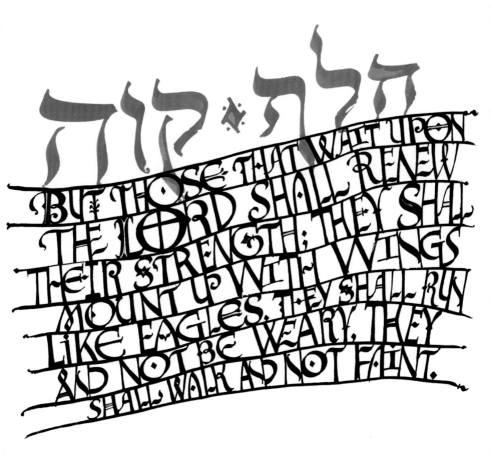

BUT THOSE THAT WAIT UPON
THE LORD SHALL RENEW
THEIR STRENGTH THEY SHALL
MOUNT UP WITH WINGS
LIKE EAGLES THEY SHALL RUN
AND NOT BE WEARY, THEY
SHALL WALK AND NOT FAINT.

And then one day, when I was 28 years old, whilst staying with friends, I slept and had a dream… There stood a man in a black hat, silhouetted against the light, tall and ominous, frightening and slim. He closed the door, and I could feel the presence as he walked around the beds back and forth, back and forth.

I woke up screaming into the cold night

"HEEEEEEEEEEEEEEEEEEEEELP………….."

My friends came running breathlessly into the room,
"What's wrong, what's wrong Tashy?"
"I had a dream, a terrible dream about the man in the black hat from when I was five years old. And… and I could feel him here in this room…. And I wanted to steal you away Les and Richard and Johannes, away… for myself."
"Wait, I will get you a hot water bottle. Wait… There, there … shhhh. Lie down, lie still, you'll be alright in a few moments."
I lay trembling and broken, fragile and anxious. My scream that had been waiting, waiting like a crouching monster had taken 23 years to come out and had emerged like a spitting tiger, a "tiger, tiger, burning bright". It had spewed out from the bowels of the earth like a volcano of venom, like a striking cobra.
Yes, I had screamed for help! The knowledge was terrifying and yet a relief. I lay down with the hot water bottle and tried to go back to uneasy sleep as I wept quietly into my pillow.

Letter I   Planet Earth
                                  3rd November 1979

Dear Doctor

I feel the need to write to you to explain the road I have
travelled for the past twenty-eight years. Perhaps after read-
ing this letter you will glean some insight into my mental
condition which may assist you in understanding how to
help me in the future.

I remember a time in my early teenage years when I wondered about the meaning of life. Was there really a god, was
there someone out there who understood me, my thoughts,
my prayers, my questions and my pain?

As a young girl I had to attend Sunday School – this was
in line with what my friends did and what was expected of
me. It was traditional and obligatory to attend church every Sunday until I graduated after confirmation. Although I
searched, I could find no-one to understand me, my thoughts,
my prayers, my questions and my pain.

I was instead dreadfully bored in confirmation classes
and couldn't wait for the time to come when I would be
free. That time did come and immediately I was confirmed
I was no longer forced to attend church. Now I could throw
off the shackles which seemed to bind my society to a rigid
and unquestioning nominal adherence to Christianity and
all that came with the package: baptism, confirmation, marriage, church attendance and the Bible. My consciousness
blossomed – I realized that there were new realms, ideas
and philosophies to discover. Yes, god was dead. I had done
my time. But now – how to find meanings in a world where
there were no gods?

I lived in a modern world. A world of motor cars with

22

smooth tailored roads for the rich, and TV, moon landings and germ warfare. A world where I could pop into the Spur every night for a burger, and where I was whisked out quickly to the beat of the trendy, racy music; a fast world of night clubs, drinking, dancing, smooching and fun.

At university I seriously began to question the 'grand narratives'. Whilst studying history I was appalled to discover just how powerful and corrupt and pervasive the church had been for nearly two thousand years. I traced a time line for myself to see graphically the rise and fall of the papacy and Rome through the centuries, and how this had influenced all decision-making down the line of the years. I identified with the Protestant reformation and its abhorrence of the Roman Catholic Church and her doctrines. This, however, just fed my rejection of the church, religion, god and the bible. How could people mindlessly follow dogmas and precepts without asking why, why, why and what for?

There were other questions which needed exploring and answering. Was it ethical for America to continue fighting in the Vietnam War? Was it any use voting? Why vote when we knew beforehand that only a portion of the electorate had the vote, and anyway we knew that the Nationalists would win the day? So why bother? In South Africa at this time there was the 'rooi gevaar' and the 'swart gevaar'; there was apartheid. And the common man believed in them, and that they needed to be defended and embraced. And a coloured boy was not allowed to sit down in a restaurant and eat with me. I was moved by the haunted faces, others and mine – but felt powerless to do anything.

But what was all this energy for? What was the meaning of life? Why was I on this planet? Where did I fit into the scheme of things? I was concerned about ME. How could I find myself and "make myself"?

I was an ordinary girl; one who conformed to the rules, who did a little homework at school – enough to get by – who read love books to escape the excruciating reality of what was out there. I behaved myself socially and attempted to be kind and unselfish, generous and caring. I remembered to say please and thank you. But I found no hooks to hang onto – money held no appeal, joining a guerrilla group to fight for a just society held no attraction for me, becoming a workaholic was too energy sapping (and what for I asked?); certainly I felt no push to join in student riots, and there was no attraction to become embroiled in religions. After all the gods were dead. Even the idea of reincarnation soon palled. What was the use of carrying on – what was it all for? Why did I feel so cut off and alone?

It was then that one day I came across Sartre's 'Age of Reason' – at last a hook to hang onto. Now I didn't feel so alone and I didn't have to commit suicide. I had found a means whereby I could work through my feelings of alienation. There was somebody out there who understood how I felt and thought and breathed and operated within my middle-class society. After that I read Camus, Kafka, Hesse, Huxley, Nietzsche, Malamud, Kazantzakis and others. Not only existentialism but other philosophies and ideas about freedom and nirvana, the ideal society, and perfection, emerged which helped me understand my world, my consciousness, my probing and questioning. At last in literature I had found companions to share my anxiety, my aloneness, my search for meaning in a crazy modern world; a world which didn't seem to understand me, one where the grand marches continued and nothing seemed to make sense or have meaning; a society which seemed to improve for an elite few and ignored the masses and the poor.

Although I was concerned with the world around me, I

was too tied up at this time of my life to even try to have much compassion for the poor – it was enough to get through a day – to survive the onslaught on non-communication, isolation, and facelessness – my strength was sapped as in the heat of summer.

But at last – Sartre – yes, I began to build my brave new world around the ideas I stole from books. Slowly my confidence grew. I was my own person – one who made the rules, followed them and carried out actions which not only I but the people in my world approved of. I was free – I shook off the shackles of indecision, depression and apathy – I emerged like a butterfly with bright colours and bold passion. The world was my garden – filled with flowers of every colour and hue and fragrance, trees, shrubs, forests, mountains and streams, skies and clouds. All was right with this paradise. And I took responsibility for my life, my decisions, my present, my past and my future; I wrote the script for my life – it was filled with worthwhile work, leisure activities, intellectual pursuits, a social life which was successful and meaningful. I wore a label across my chest: "One hell of a fulfilled and successful human being". I am still haunted by my friend's words: "You are a *very* together person".

I travelled across the seas to explore the other ends of the earth. I asked from life only that I remain healthy in mind and body – I went to experience the riches other societies had to offer. Here I was plunged into a world of consumerism, technology, industrialization, art and music, fast foods of every choice and type, abundant products for the choosing. For the first time in my life I was able to buy shoes that fitted my large feet – I chose from myriads of colours, shapes and fashions. I flew around Europe exploring all that modernity had to offer: Switzerland with her super cleanliness, organisation, banks and chocolates, France with her art, music, cuisine and wines, Holland with her permissiveness, tulips and drugs, Denmark with her feminism. Romania and her communism, and Germany with her automobile industry and the Autobahn; a fantastic jet-setting world of high tech, democracy and politics, choices, abundance, leisure and sex; a cosmopolitan world where Jewish, Arab, Malaysian, Jamaican, British, Pakistani, Australian and American men abounded.

I returned home to the desert of South-West Africa. It was here that I studied the poem by William Blake called 'London'. In the quiet and stillness of the desert I reflected on my time in London and overseas.

I wander thro' each charter'd street,
Near where the chartered Thames does flow.
And mark in every face I meet
Marks of weakness, marks of woe.

In every cry of every man,
In every Infant's cry of fear,
In every voice: in every ban,
The mind-forged manacles I hear.

How the Chimney-sweeper's cry
Every blackning church appalls;
And the hapless Soldier's sigh
Runs in blood down Palace walls.

But most thro' midnight streets I hear
How the youthful Harlot's curse
Blasts the new-born Infant's tear,

And blights with plagues the Marriage hearse.[2]

This poem was to have a profound influence on my life. I questioned once again the "chartered" role of industry and progress and technology in our modern world. The "mind-forged manacles" were evident everywhere where men and women were in bondage to the grand narratives. The church was indeed "blackened", both literally and figuratively, the soldier went to war without questioning why. Only the harlot seemed to survive the chartered world.

Despite all this I tried to live a life with meaning. I had found myself. And as the warm winds of the Namib Desert enveloped me, I was able to affirm that my existence was part of a tapestry of meaning and purpose. I was able to live with myself and embrace my loneliness. Somehow my loneliness had become my solitude.

It was around this time that I wondered if there was such a thing as "love". What was it? Could it help me and others? Well – perhaps love was remembering to smile, to say hello, to acknowledge another. Yes, a possibility was love. And what about real love with a man? Having been so moved by the harlot in Blake's poem, I decided to "give myself away to love".

Oh, the confidence and courage of youth – the sheer joy of living with abandonment in a world of freedom and enlightenment. But pride, they say, goes before a fall. All was well when suddenly everything crashed around me. I lost sight of the meanings, the responsibility for myself.

This is why I write to you doctor. I find that my existential existence cannot contain me anymore. It was not adequate to sustain me through a love affair – one where I could not live with my own guilt. Why guilt? Was I not beyond guilt?

---

2   https://genius.com/William-blake-london-annotated § 1794

Why did I have this over-active conscience? I thought I had made the world work for me, that I would be able to rise above anything – but I was wrong.

Now I am certified and confined to a closed ward and I don't know how to rebuild my life – the old stories don't work anymore, the ideas and the freedom and the taking responsibility for myself. Do you really know what it's like here Doc? Do you understand my anguish and my pain? Let me tell you about life in the here and now.

Here is my poem:

WARD
Feet shuffling, faces distorted with pain
Meaninglessness at its finest
Incessant lighting of cigarettes to keep away the bore-
dom, the thoughts of tomorrow and the sameness of it all
Shuffling, smoking, pain,
Thoughts, meaninglessness
And the noise is unbearable
Psychotic sounds and keys being rattled, doors noisily
opened and shut
Opened and shut
Why?

I seem to be back where I started. There is the apathy,
depression and meaninglessness. So can you help me doc? I
am twenty-eight years old. I have fought enough battles for
one lifetime. I am broken and bleeding, dreadfully scarred
and re-labelled an imbecile. I am an island. Is this the end or
is there something else out there perhaps?

Can anybody help me?

Morningside
The old man died
And no-one cried
They simply turned away

And when he died
He left a table made of nails and pride
And with his hands,
He carved these words inside

'For my children'

Morning light
Morning bright
I spent the night
With dreams that make you weep
Morning time
Wash away the sadness
From these eyes of mine
For I recall the words an old man signed
'For my children'

[Spoken:]
And the legs were shaped with his hands
And the top made of oaken wood
And the children
That sat around this great table
Touched it with their laughter
Ah, and that was good

Morningside
An old man died
And no-one cried
He surely died alone
And truth is sad
For not a child would claim the gift he had
The words he carved became his epitaph
'For my children'[3]

---

3   Neil Diamond: Morningside: www.azlyrics.com §Released: 1972

as a man
thinks
to himself,
so will he be.

ΜΕΤΆΝΟΙΑ

PROVERBS 23:7

Dear Mom

I have to share some things with you now as time has (after 43 years) healed all the hurts and pains. Everything has become beautiful in its time.

You rejected me a number of times which caused me grave trauma. I am writing to you so that everybody who reads this letter will realize what happens to babies in the womb.

First, you rejected me when you realised you were pregnant with me – it was a couple of months after my sister was born. I understand … but …

Then you wanted an abortion so rejected me a second time.

Then you went to a fortune teller who told you that you would have a baby boy. I was named Nate in the womb. But you never realized that a curse was put on me – a grievous, dangerous curse. I was Rosemary's Baby!!

I could never tell you this for I knew you would not altogether understand. And so, the devil came to claim me when I was five.

And then I had to fight for my femininity when I was born and as I grew up. No longer Nate but now Natasha.

That is why I totally rejected YOU. I was tied to you and had to first break free from my bondages before I could love you again. Do you understand Mom?

Love Natasha

One tear drizzled out of her left eye and fell onto her pillow
She remembered her mother; so beautiful, so soft, silky, sweet smelling and serious,
Beloved wife to John and mother of three
How often did that one tear fall?
Often as she recalled the past and the folly and the fury
Of their relationship
Bound together by an umbilical cord that never was severed
Except in death. But yet not as the tight knot is still there because of our love for one another
Again, one tear drizzled out of her left eye as she walked the streets of London.
Remembering, remembering, remembering.
I trust I will see you again, Mutti, to apologize and say thank you.

Dear Dad

My rock star, my beacon of light. Thank you for your amazing Daddyship. But I rejected you and even hated you when there was nothing left of me but a Belsen soul and body. I had nothing left to give, only hate and rejection. So, you see everything has come full circle for all of us. Mom rejected me and I rejected Mom and I hated you. But you left everything to me and to my siblings. Everything was 'For my children'.

Thank you Ol' Bean.

Love Tashy

Dear Pooh and Boy

You are still my favourite people in the world. Thank you, Boy, for your charisma and brilliant intellect, which you have used for the healing of the marginalized, the rejected. You are my Admired One. And Pooh, you are always so completely honest with me and I love you for this. Our sisterhood is so real, so blatantly brilliant. Thank you for your motherhood to Kyle and Madam, such unconditional love to them and to all. You are a real Martha, but so beloved and Madam is Martha like you, the best mothers in the world to little Sophia. And thank you Sam, for helping me with this essay. You are the most incredible inspiration and I admire your creative spirit. You are a dazzling gem so welcome to the family.

You have all helped me through the storms and overflowing rivers of life. Thank you.

Love Tashy

Nightwatchman

He swept in with the swirling leaves that cold,
Autumn night.
Like a dark, ethereal clouded shadow looming.
An intruder bursting into the ward – how did he break into this dark, fetid prison?
He came to bring the light, to tell me there was a devil roaring outside.
I trembled, but he so gentle humble, so consoling, so comforting.
John the Baptist come to visit 2 000 years later.
A friend to all, poor but giving everything away, consoling the inconsolable, offering tea and Jesus.
This great, humble prophet who became my friend 'inside'.

Planet Earth
3rd November 1979

Dear Doctor

I am twenty-eight years old. I have fought enough battles for one lifetime. I am dreadfully broken and bleeding, scarred and re-labelled an imbecile. Is this the end or is there something else out there perhaps?

Can anybody help me?

No – there is no-one, Nemo, Nemo, Nemo.

Good-night, sweet (princess);
And flights of angels sing thee to thy rest.[4]

---

4   William Shakespeare: Hamlet: Act 5: Scene 2: www.goodreads.com
§ Released 1603

THE TOMB AND THE ISLAND

4th November 1979 – 30th March 2000

Dear Teacher

This is when I retreated into the cave, where I spent the dark nights of brain-washing and excruciating torture of my soul. Then when all was finished, I lay down in the shrouded cave and covered myself in swaddling clothes and slept the deep, deep sleep of death.

I do not know for how many years I slept, but one morning I woke – my mind was filled with light. I opened my eyes to see the golden shafts of sunlight striking in at the opening of the tomb. The stone must have been rolled away. I got up, slipped on jeans and a T-shirt and some sandals and put on a hat. I tiptoed to the entrance to the tomb. The light was too bright. I felt like a chicken which had just hatched out of its egg – pink, featherless and rather ugly, or was I perhaps a little "joey" – new-born – minute and hairless ready to make that incredible journey to the pouch and teat? No – I was more like a butterfly just emerged from the cocoon – fragile, vulnerable, with silky wings still wet and dewy.

A shadow fell across the opening. "Hello Natasha, I'm Myange and I shall be your companion and guide until you are ready to face the world once more."

"Hello Myange, pleased to meet you," I said.

Myange led me into an enchanted garden and showed me all the verdant trees and flowering shrubs and animals. She made and provided the choicest breads and the finest wines, with delicious nuts and vegetables and fruit to eat. And my education began.

Myange taught me about philosophy, history and all the

religions of the world, about politics and medicine and how one must be careful about the road one chooses to follow. She related to me how she had often chosen the wrong paths and been terribly wounded and scarred in battle. She also told me about the society "out there" where I would have to return one day and described to me the different technologies and ways of mankind. We would sit for hours chatting about life and the big questions of the world.

She taught me chess, backgammon and whist, and we often spent time playing scrabble, monopoly and the crystal bead game. To wile away the hours Myange and I would go for long walks along the beach beyond the garden and talk about people, society and the meaning of life. We walked the mountains together. In the early mornings we would go swimming in the waves and at night we pored over books and manuscripts. At times we would separate and spend time alone, meditating, thinking, imagining. She was my teacher and I a keen learner.

One day, Myange said it was time for me to return to planet earth. I didn't want to accept the truth that I would now have to leave my beloved mentor.

"Why can't I stay with you?" I pleaded.

"Because it is the time," said Myange, "and because it is the time, you must go. I will take you to the bottom of the garden, where the sand meets the sea. Don't look back. Be strong and very courageous and go into the future bravely."

I was sad to take that final walk with Myange. But I obeyed and plunged into the cold water without looking back.

Dear Myange

Our friendship was like David and Jonathan's. You and I shared the deepest secrets over the years. And we laughed and cursed so much together and lambasted one another – but love overshadowed all the dark shadows under our eyes. You taught me so much and I can never thank you adequately.

You prepared me for fighting battles.

Take care sweet friend.

Tashy

Thy will be done.

γενηθήτω

"Argghh!" I woke up with a start. It was all a dream. That reminded me – one of my favourite songs was about a dream. I switched on the CD player whilst I whisked into the shower, washed my hair, brushed my teeth and then got ready for a new day.

I have a dream, a song to sing
To help me cope with anything
If you see the wonder of a fairy tale
You can take the future even if you fail

I believe in angels
Something good in everything I see
I believe in angels
When I know the time is right for me
I'll cross the stream
I have a dream

I have a dream, a fantasy
To help me through reality
And my destination makes it worth the while
Pushing through the darkness still another mile
I believe in angels
Something good in everything I see

I believe in angels
When I know the time is right for me
I'll cross the stream

I have a dream
I'll cross the stream
I have a dream
I have a dream, a song to sing
To help… [5]

---

5   Abba   ~   www.lyrics.com/lyric/33402173/Susan+Boyle/
I+Have+a+Dream: Released § 1979

In the year 2000 I rested and became a celibate person.

But I had a fantasy

I want to meet a man from the other side. Straight and tall, strong and courageous. I want to wrap him around me so that there is no more of him. He is completely inside, warm and soft, gentle and probing. I have this fantasy of him and me on the warm sands of time where pleasure never ends and where there is no pain. Where we can look one another in the eyes and say, "Be forever mine."

Take this fantasy Lord as I cast it away into the cosmos. "Go away and find some place to settle where you can consummate your love and lust on a foreign sandy shore. And worry not about the shame at home."
I have a fantasy.

This played in the background as I carefully put on my make-up and dried my hair.

Well, I only had a half hour before work. I was excited – today I would have the privilege of interviewing members of the Master Class and hoped to discuss questions about post-modernism.

MASTER CLASS

University

4 p.m.

"Here we are then, on time for Master Class. Let's start with Piet Weidemann."

"Hello, everybody, can we hit the road. Thanks. Thank you everyone."

"Piet, you are facilitating this section of the course dealing with post-modernism. How would you describe the post-modern condition?"

"Well, first of all, there is the strong influence from the existentialist school in post-modernism. One is able to step out of oneself, begin self-therapy and decide where one is going. We have overwhelming choices today where change is always an exciting possibility. There is also the added spice of risk and new opportunities. Our options are open until the day we die and even in death we have some choices. So we can support the Heidegger position and say that we are writing the narrative for our lives ourselves."

"Yes – thank you – and what else strikes you about post-modernism?"

"Today we are almost obsessed with the body. Do you remember the hand-out I gave you on the types of alternative therapies available to the modern subject? Everything from reflexology, to yoga to Tai Chi. Although in the past we have concentrated rather on the mind, it seems that we now concentrate heavily on the body. I think today we have gone over the top focusing particularly on the body beautiful."

"But Piet, it seems to me that man is still constantly searching for some kind of meaning, some kind of acknowledgement of his presence. He seems to be obsessing about trying to find truth even if it means that he has to beautify and placate the body first."

"Possibly. But I expect that man will never stop searching for meaning, Natasha."

"The thing that horrifies me is that all of us who peddle and push and pant at the Health and Racket Club, seem to be staying on the spot. This seems to be a metaphor for the way we get nowhere with the body, Piet."

"OK Natasha, let's change tack and try another angle. We can see the post-modern spirit in some of the new buildings which have been erected in the past few years in our city. Buildings are iconic and therefore a reflection of post-modernism. I find the juxtaposition of for example, the Marie Koopmans De-Wet Huis and The Pinnacle – the aluminium structure next to it – rather playful and fascinating, almost caring in the way they are aware of one another. The aluminium triangles are talking to the smaller triangles in the older building. And yes, I think the architects created something rather pleasing. This is perhaps part of the human spirit which we could possibly call post-modernism."

"I would like to add that post-modernism contains a hesitance. It is not tangible and certainly will not produce a state of nirvana. After all we are too informed and far more aware of the problems we face in our world today than people did in history."

"Thank you Piet. I have Mike Lotter on the phone – architect of The Pinnacle. Mike, you've been listening to this seminar over the phone – would you like to comment?"

"Well Natasha, I'm not sure that I see these two buildings talking to one another as a post-modern idiom. The Pinnacle is a building that tries to respond to its context – take into account the building structures around it – and respond to people's space. To say that it's post-modern – I don't think so. But it depends on what one defines as the post-modern spirit. A lot of the time post-modern structures are brightly coloured and influenced by Graves. May I say a lot of our response was almost humanist; having to do with people's space, taking into account Koopmans De-Wet Huis and trying to capture different elements and lines; put something next to it that is separate and yet complementary. Does that answer your question Natasha?"

"Well, sort of. I think that both you and Piet may be correct in your interpretations. After all in post-modernism we are able to respond in a number of different ways to a situation. Perhaps this will come out later in one of our other interviews."

"Thanks very much Mike Lotter for joining us today."

"Johan, may I turn to you now please. You seem to have had quite a lot to say in this Master Class. Would you call yourself a post-modernist, and why?"

"Yes, absolutely, I definitely consider myself to be a post-modernist. Take the situation in Ethiopia. I don't care a fuck about Ethiopia, or about Africa for that matter; it has to start looking after itself. I don't care and I don't feel guilty. I will choose the charities I want to support here at home. That's post-modernism for you."

"Johan, do you think you're maybe suffering from burn-out? You know, too many demands on your psyche and your purse – from exhaustion perhaps?"

"You're absolutely right, Natasha, I am exhausted by the demands being made on me both psychologically and financially."

"Thank you Johan."

"Margaret, you're one of the students with us in this Master Class. How do you see post-modernism affecting you as a teacher-trainer and student?"

"I think the main thing is for the teachers to create situations for the learners to participate and experience their own learning. It's moving away from content-based lessons and activities and from my perspective as a maths teacher – to give children the opportunity to learn, and encounter maths content in real situations – move away from formal groups on the mat – and try to incorporate skills training in a much more fun way. We need to try to present stuff in a fun way."

"Well Margaret, how does this link with post-modernism?"

"One must think in terms of a non-modernist curriculum. There are aspects of outcomes-based education that are post-modern – we need to challenge the modernist structures in our schools. Our curriculum may not be a complete post-modernist curriculum but it needs to chip away and challenge the modernist position."

"Margaret, what about you? Are you a post-modernist?"

"I think I am."

"In what way?"

"I think I do not, even intentionally, do this – but I find many responses to one situation – similar to Mike and Piet's different ways of looking at buildings. I find I have many solutions to a problem. It is an element of the work I do with teachers that I try to solve those problems from many different perspectives. I have no set way as it were."

"That's really interesting Margaret. Many thanks for your input."

"Let's turn to you J.C. Thanks for agreeing to do this interview. I know you've got a hectic schedule and that you have a run planned for later so we'll try to be as pithy as we can in this short space of time."

"Firstly, would you consider yourself a post-modernist?"

"Well, not really, Natasha. Although I like to think of myself as a free individual, making choices and taking risks, even charting my own path under my Father's guidance, my focus and mission is to bring in a Kingdom which focuses on the unselfishness of the individual, and not on the type of immoral and self-interested individualism which is the mark of what I would term an alienating and 'alien' philosophy. One has to retain one's integrity, honesty and righteousness to work in my organization. This doesn't exactly tie in with serial monogamy, widespread corruption and the high stress and suicide rate of this post-modern era. I need to emphasize that we also live as part of a community in our Kingdom."

"One needs to have a balance between reaching one's potential as an individual and living in and supporting others in a community."

"So you still have high hopes for your way of life?"

"Absolutely. I reckon that post-modernism will come and go like all the other philosophies down the centuries. Let me quote some statistics. The church is expanding at the rate of 7.2% a year over and above the population explosion figures. It's the only religion that is growing by winning converts. I think Christianity will outstrip post-modernism and any other religion or philosophy and ultimately we hope that the Kingdom will come in all its fullness on the planet."

"Well, that's quite a disclosure. Many thanks J.C."

"A pleasure. By the way, Natasha, are you a post-modernist?"

"Well, in some ways yes, and in some ways no. You see, I like the idea of being an individual who can pursue her own potential and come out on top, but on the other hand I also have a foot in the traditional camp which sides with old-fashioned values. I feel there has to be a base, a structure to society. There should be a striving to hold the family together, otherwise there is just a break-down of all we hold dear and clearly a kind of anarchy. One needs to achieve a balance between post-modernism and traditionalism in order to make a success of life I think.

I'm definitely someone who believes in self-therapy and self-reflection though and I think commitment is an important word I would like to mention."

"Yes, I liked Piet's idea and example of the two buildings caring for each other. It has a ring of sincerity about it. Well, I have to go. Thanks class for the interest."

"Thanks. Enjoy your run in the forest."

"Well, would anybody else in the class like to add a snippet before we end this discussion?"

"No? Well then, everybody, that almost concludes the class. Perhaps as an aside I would like to add that if post-modernism enhances the imagination of the individual and society as a whole, which would enable us to solve our problems on this planet creatively, we would no doubt all embrace this quest for a better life for all. Is it possible that we see an inkling of this imaginative spirit in the wonderful interplay between the different buildings which Piet showed us in the photographs last week?"

"I'll leave you with that thought."

"Thanks everybody."

"Well, Piet, I offer you this pastiche for your perusal. Do respond in the same vein. Many thanks."

Sincerely

Natasha Anderson
a.k.a. "Purple Empress"

Dear Pappie, Boetie and Complete Mentor
Welcome into this your story. You were there from the be-
ginning but I did not always know that.
I only found you later in the saga, and I am still finding you
Three. The mystical universal everything.
You have now given me all things and an inheritance be-
yond description.

Love from your Beloved

and you shall call his name Jesus

JESUS

Matthew 1:21

for he will save his people from their sins

Letter III

'Come to me, all you who are weary and burdened and I will give you rest. Take my yoke upon you and learn from me for I am gentle and humble in heart, and you will find rest for your souls. For my yoke is easy and my burden is light.'[6]

From a distance the world looks blue and green
And the snow-capped mountains so white
From a distance the ocean meets the stream
And the eagle takes to flight

From a distance there is harmony
And it echoes through the land
It's the voice of hope
It's the voice of peace
It's the voice of every man

From a distance we all have enough
And no one is in need
And there are no guns, no bombs and no disease
No hungry mouths to feed

From a distance we are instruments
Marching in a common band
Playing songs of hope
Playing songs of peace
They are the songs of every man

---

6   The Bible: New International Version: Matthew 11: 28-30

God is watching us
God is watching us
God is watching us from a distance

From a distance you look like my friend
Even though we are at war
From a distance I can't comprehend
What all this fighting's for
From a distance there is harmony
And it echoes through the land
And it's the hope of hopes
It's the love of loves
It's the heart of every man
It's the hope of hopes
It's the love of loves
It's the heart of every man
This is the song of every man

God is watching us
God is watching
God is watching us from a distance[7]

---

7   [Julie Gold: From a distance: www.songfacts.com/lyrics/bette-midler/from-a-distance: Released 1990]

קחצי

Then Abraham
fell on his face
and laughed.

GENESIS 17:17

Claremont

Dear Piet

I have *just* returned from class and turned on the computer to sit down and write to you about the course and me. It seems appropriate to write the last letter to you about my feelings and reflections and ideas concerning the course of the past four months – especially since you have accompanied me through my journey and its pain and my ultimate metamorphosis.

I have indeed been fortunate, for this is my second year of doing *Teaching and the Modern Condition*. If you remember, last year I did the course but de-registered because of pressure of work. Well, that was partially true, but actually the thing that really got to me was the gigantic essay of 6000 words which we were required to produce on the different aspects of the course. It was all just too much for me – I couldn't face the readings, which I found too difficult, and I panicked about producing something worthwhile which would enable me to qualify for doing the Masters proper. I felt as though I was part of an oppressive nightmare. But what a privilege that I was able to attend the lectures of all four courses despite the fact that I was no longer registered. Many thanks.

So when I re-registered this year at the very last minute because the university could not accommodate me in the Mathematics Further Diploma in Education, I was somewhat apprehensive, but also somewhat prepared – after all I had taken part in the dress rehearsal and now was to be the performance. However, I must say that my fears have been allayed and I have realised that as a learner I sometimes learn things like mathematics bonds very quickly but when it comes to philosophy I needed to have done that extra year. And the fact that I have been able to express myself in letters has been a bonus – for apart from eating, letter and story writing are my favourite activities. I think if I had been faced with another 6000 worder I would have found an excuse to de-register again. So again many thanks for the creative way in which we have been allowed to respond to the subject matter.

These two years of the course for me have been life changing. Especially as what you did this year included some similar readings, but different ones too, which I found enriching. I have been a teacher in schools for some 24 years, and a teacher trainer for four years, and know at this stage in my life that my headmistress was quite right to choose teaching for me and not veterinary science. I have pooled every resource I possess and some which I didn't even know were part of my character and personality into my profession, and have had the most outstanding rewards from both what I and my students have achieved. There is nothing in the whole world that can beat that sense of exciting, adrenaline pumping fire which one gets from interacting and working with and teaching students. It's a feeling only teachers know about, I think, because you don't get it in any other profession.

And so I continue to study, to learn, to reflect and to debate, and this course – over a period of two years – has afforded me such an opportunity.

This course has been wonderfully refreshing, a time aside to see what is going on in the bigger world of education and of life. It has been a time to reflect on the past, to put things in perspective and to plan for the future.

What can one say about the eclectic and electric selection of subjects and readings which you both chose for the course? Very exciting, challenging, modern and post-modern, sometimes alarming and sometimes alluring. I have been on a journey from the centre to the periphery of the earth; I have been 'around the world in eighty days'. Now that I am on the edge of the planet, I need to see where my path will take me next. I have a blurred vision at the moment and hope that this will be more focussed by the time I end this letter.

During this course I have re-lived the horrors and blights of modernism – being certified and becoming a vegetable. I was re-born and tutored for the 21st century only to then emerge into a post-modern milieu which I playfully challenged and judged and finally "spat out of my mouth". So, from my perspective, on the outside, where to now?

Let me get into a space module and lift-off into space so that I have a bird's eye view. I am looking down on the Blue Planet.

'All the world's a stage, and all the men and women merely players' comes to mind.'[8]

What am I going to do with my old and new knowledge in the light of this course? Where am I going to next? How am I going to change the planet? What script am I going to write for the world? How can I begin to discern the tiny figures and the configurations through the opaque blur of the clouds?

So as I look down from my space-ship, there is much that I see which I do not like. I do not like the greed, the ghettos, the selfishness, the pride, the abuse, the violence, the drugs, the hate and the killing. I see a world where the majority of the population is suffering from deprivation of one sort

---

8   William Shakespeare: As you like it: Act 2: Scene 7: www.poets. org/poem/ you-it-act-ii-scene-vii-all-worlds-stage § published 1623

or another, and yet there is a minority who have more than more than enough. I see people crying and people dying. I see the rich in their plush, white leather seats. I see a class at a university where people are talking about post-modernism. They play around with ideas and words. They laugh and banter as they seek for meanings and for satisfaction. They don't realize that they are admiring themselves, admiring their playfulness, their ability to think and challenge and change. And they are so wonderfully self-centred and unbelievably arrogant. It's the self-admiration society at work and at play in the fields of the world. It's all in the name of the game, I suppose. What else could they talk about in this Master Class in a post-modern setting, at a post-modern university, in a post-modern world? After all, does it matter that 84% of the population is part of a world where it doesn't matter a damn about deconstruction and playfulness and self-gratification and selfishness of the other 16% who are so busy placating their bodies and their minds that it stinks.

I vomit when I think of Johan in his incredible arrogance proclaiming that he is a "fucking" post-modernist and to hell with Africa and the rest. I cringe when I think that you blandly and calmly claim to be one who plays the intellectual game with ideas and concepts – "Let's not take things so seriously. And let's leave the problem. It doesn't matter, does it? The thing is to play at it and then leave it." I am amazed at such an "intelligent" bunch of so-called adults "mooning and spooning" over every word that is spoken by the "gurus" of post-modernism and the similar mouthing of students around the room.

Get real people. There is a world out there that is screaming in the pain of abandonment. Get your fannies into gear and go into the world to find out what it is really like. There you will find pain, and humiliating humanity begging for a stompie, people so filthy, so deprived and depraved that you would not believe it. Leave your white leather upholstery and venture into

the world of the poor,
the world of the imbecile,
the world of the disabled,
the world of the addict,
the world of the psychotic,
the world of the maimed,
the world of the raped,

because this is the real world and this is the world we have to re-build, nurture, mend and heal now and in the next generation – otherwise there will no longer be a place for us and those who come after. And we cannot do it alone; we need each other. So abandon your own desires and wants and "have to haves" and self-indulgences and step into the unknown. Take a risk, a chance, give everything away to and for the world.

You will find some comfort in so doing. Because it is only when we realize that it is we who need healing that we are able to reach out to others to heal them. So I would implore that you put aside your self-absorption, ideas and agendas and start talking about how to serve and save this planet and the billions of people who need us.

As I look down from the module, I realize suddenly that it is only because I have had two years of intellectual conversation and dialogue that I am able to see through the blur of the clouds. I hear the voices whispering to me – they are the voices of the people. They plead and beg and entreat and wail. The clouds seem to be clearing; I can see the colours of the blue and green living, exquisite planet. There *is* only

one way to go forward.
     The module has landed. I am here to save the world.
     Who is going to save it with me?

                    Sincerely

                    Natasha Anderson

καλός

I am the good shepherd
I know my sheep
and my sheep know me
~just as the Father knows me
and I know the Father ~
and I lay down my life
✠ for the sheep. ✠

John 10:14-15

God is watching us, God is watching us,
God is watching us, from a distance.
From a distance, you look like my friend,
Even though we are at war.
From a distance, I can't comprehend,
What all this war is for.
What we need is love and harmony,
Let it echo through the land.
It's the hope of hopes, it's the love of loves,
It's the heart of everyone.

Sing out, Songs of Hope,
Sing out, Songs of Freedom,
Sing out, Songs of Love,
Sing out, Songs of Peace,
Sing out, Songs of Justice,
Sing out, Songs of Harmony,
Sing out, Songs of Love,
Sing out, Everyone,
Sing out, Songs of Hope,
Sing out, Songs of Freedom,
Sing out, Songs of Love,
Sing out, Songs of Peace,
Sing out, Songs of Justice,
Sing out, Songs of Harmony,
Sing out, sing about Love
Sing out, Everyone.
Sing out.[9]

---

9   Cliff Richard: From a distance: www.metrolyrics.com/from-a-distance-lyrics-cliff-richard.html § Released 1990

Autumn in Coventry, 2016

Nothing is more beautiful than Autumn.
When leaves in whirls and twirls and curls
Float down so softly, so silently to the
Wedding floor of this earth of majesty.
The colours dazzle and razzle and tangle
And burst into songs of sunlight, sunset evenings
And summer greens.

Like a wedding confetti carpet…

What prophecy is this for the bride as she sleeps
Waiting for the kiss of the Beloved?
This Autumn in Coventry, one of the
Chosen valleys of **a thousand dreams.**

Dear Tashy

I am writing this letter to you, to me, to myself. Behold, I was shaped in iniquity, I was in the abyss, I was cast out into an open field, in the day that I was born. But I was brought up out of a horrible pit, out of miry clay, and my feet were set upon a rock, and my goings were established.

Thank you to my friends and family, strangers and fellow inmates, who carried me and nurtured me through the torments, the pain and the terrors. Thank you to nurses and doctors and medicine which kept me sane and enabled me to work these past 43 years. Thank you.

I have described this journey beyond the stars, beyond the clouds, beyond the infinite. Only with the help of humankind and my Beloved was this possible. And now we wait for "le dénouement".

Love from Natasha

P.S. I revel in the valley as I wait patiently.

Breedekloof Valley July 2022

I don't walk the streets no more - I walk the vineyards. Today alone. In the cool afternoon with sharp air and fresh sky vistas. But with the golden and black Labradors – my favourite times.

The clouds declare the annals of history in half sphere sweeping dome: the glory cumulus, the snowy, grey, browny mink coat above the Brandwag.

The silver linings as the sun drowns in the west. All holding promises. I am alone in the windy, waiting valley – waiting for history to unfold. Unfold into a Midsummer Night's Dream.

Share this valley and this dream with me…

Blue Heavens August 2022

Soon Spring! I walk and dance through the vineyards with the Labs. Cat's tails like golden sheaves bowing like Joseph's technicolour dream. Tall, lush, emerald grasses – straight roads through the trimmed vines. Fairest blue blaze in the distance with shadowy folds and the Brandwag like a sentinel keeping watch over the sacred valley, like Gabriel. Fecund smells of loamy soil and detritus and white daisies and sour sierings. Miggies like orbs in the sunlight.

The children come to greet the dogs and brown eyes meet blue. Sweet children of perfect promise in this pregnant, expectant valley.

THE FUTURE COMING TO THE FUTURE

IMAGINATION

According to Kearney, there is today in our postmodern world an impasse as far as imagination is concerned. According to him, there will be no more leaps of imagination in the future. Could we change the word imagination and use another word for the artistic pastiche we now see in our galleries and postmodern contexts?

Has the time come for us to play and re-create in the postmodern era, rather than keep inventing the brand new? Even Science Fiction is all a pastiche of what has been invented and thought about before.

We waited for the apocalypse at the end of the last century. But what if it comes soon ... and sooner rather than later? What if it comes now? This Spring, this October, this Cape Town?

Then we will work and play with divine inspiration in the fields of the Lord, we will take the time to examine what has gone before and re-live and re-invent using modern technology. Together we will enjoy rebuilding and remaking and perfecting and creating "afresh" using all that has come and has gone in the past, to build a world of beauty and wholeness. We will create a world without shadows and without darkness. We will make a reality of that which we have imagined and fancied. And a house for everybody, with windows and a door and a chimney and garden and a swing and we will live happily ever after.......... For ever and ever.

It doesn't matter that there will be no more leaps of the imagination. We have everything we need on the planet to re-create and live on Planet Earth.

FACT

I slept, I awoke. I was a butterfly. Slowly my wings dried and became firm and strong. I was ready to fly.

And it was here in the garden that I met my Prince. He was tall and dark, slim and handsome, a real Prince. And he said, "See! The winter is past; the rains are over and gone. Flowers appear on the earth, the season of singing has come, the cooing of doves is heard in our land. The fig tree forms its early fruit; the blossoming vines spread their fragrance. Arise, come, my darling; my beautiful one, come with me."
(Song of Songs 2: 12, 13, Holy Bible)

As I walk down the aisle to my handsome Prince, to the altar, to the throne, I remember Sleeping Beauty. She woke up from a dream. I remember the Ugly Duckling. Today I am a swan. All glorious am I, my gown interwoven with gold. In embroidered garments I am led to my Prince. My virgin companions follow me. They are led in with joy and gladness; they enter the palace of the King.

And the world and the nations rejoice and they dance on the streets that are golden.

Jesus said to him,

"I am the way,
and the truth,
and the life;
no one comes
to the Father,
but by me."

John 14:6